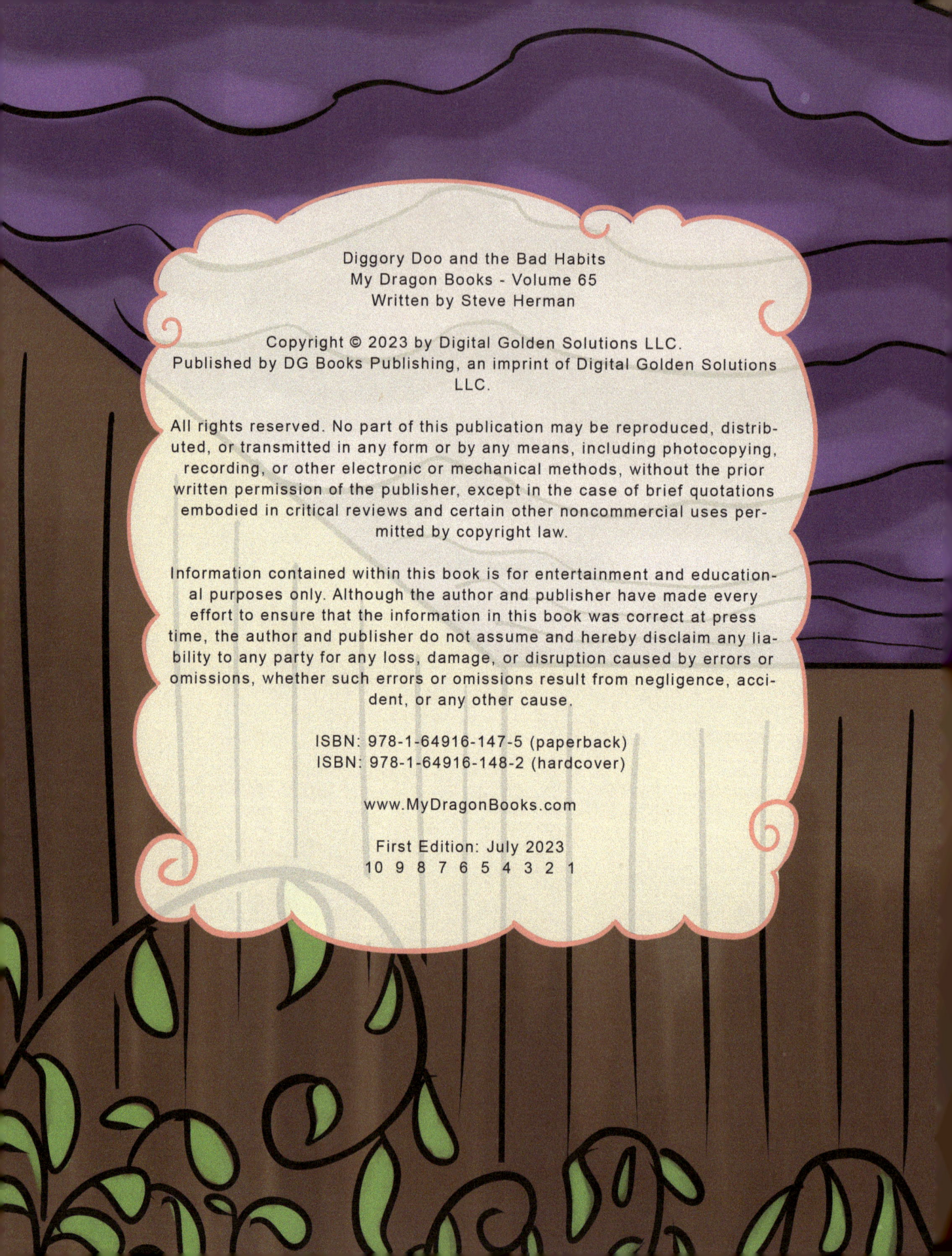

Diggory Doo and the Bad Habits
My Dragon Books - Volume 65
Written by Steve Herman

Copyright © 2023 by Digital Golden Solutions LLC.
Published by DG Books Publishing, an imprint of Digital Golden Solutions LLC.

All rights reserved. No part of this publication may be reproduced, distributed, or transmitted in any form or by any means, including photocopying, recording, or other electronic or mechanical methods, without the prior written permission of the publisher, except in the case of brief quotations embodied in critical reviews and certain other noncommercial uses permitted by copyright law.

Information contained within this book is for entertainment and educational purposes only. Although the author and publisher have made every effort to ensure that the information in this book was correct at press time, the author and publisher do not assume and hereby disclaim any liability to any party for any loss, damage, or disruption caused by errors or omissions, whether such errors or omissions result from negligence, accident, or any other cause.

ISBN: 978-1-64916-147-5 (paperback)
ISBN: 978-1-64916-148-2 (hardcover)

www.MyDragonBooks.com

First Edition: July 2023
10 9 8 7 6 5 4 3 2 1

A good night's sleep is a habit that will keep you feeling fine, But Diggory stayed up late, which made it hard to rise and shine.

Diggory Doo likes soda, burgers, fries, and cakes.
My dragon didn't realize the difference diet makes.

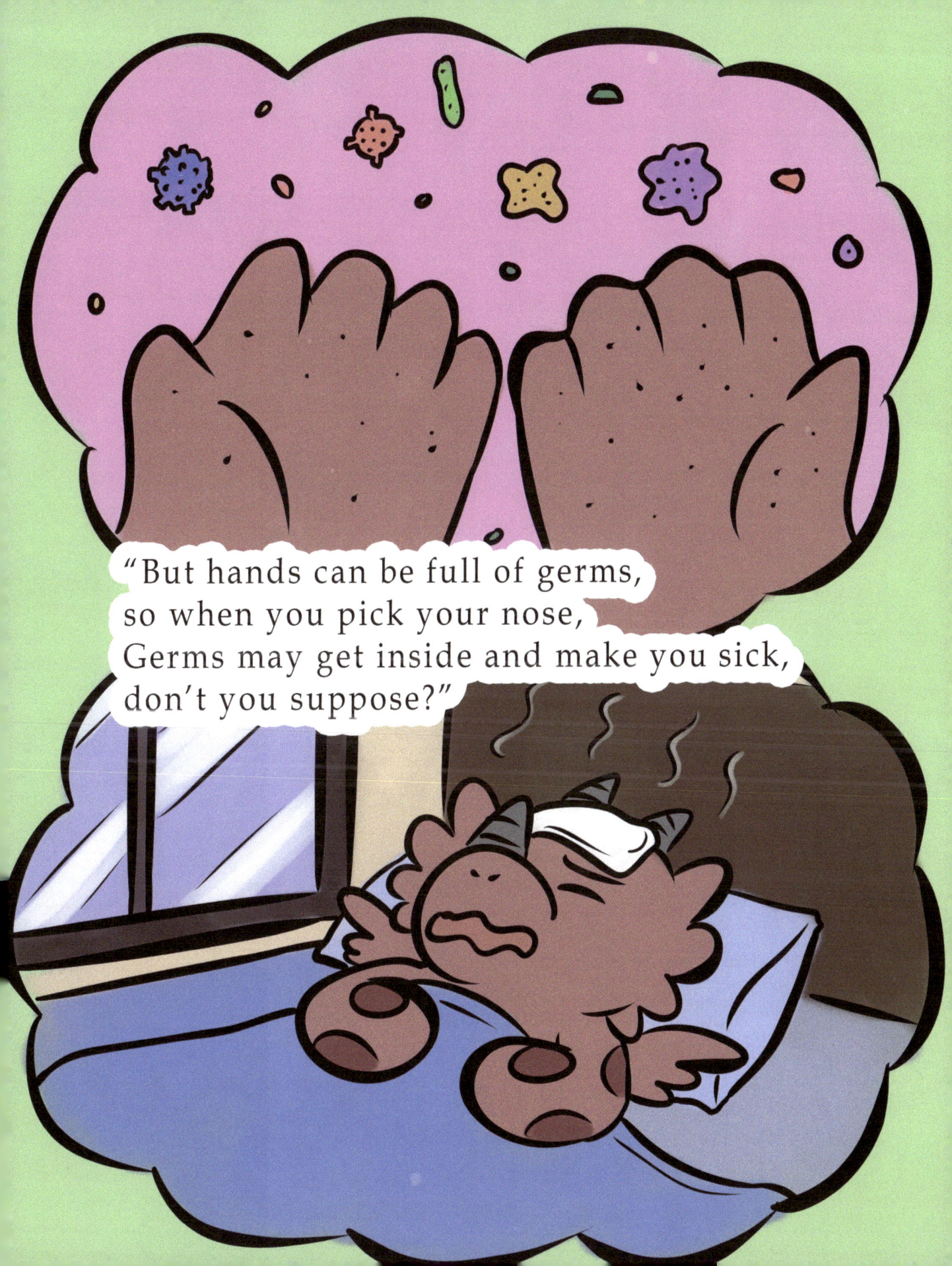

"You look at screens too much," I said, "and all of us agree
That if you didn't stare at screens so much, how happy you would be."

"If you go to bed on time –
Let this be a warning –
You will feel much better
when you wake up in the morning."

"You will wake up right on time, and then you will be able To have a healthy breakfast with your family at the table."

Now Diggory does not pick his nose; his nails are safe from chewing, And he's more fun to be around since he's not always viewing...

A screen for hours and hours. Now he plays with us instead, And he also broke the habit of going late to bed.

He's up on time, eats breakfast, and does not miss the bus;
He's eating healthy and stays awake in class, so the teacher doesn't fuss.

  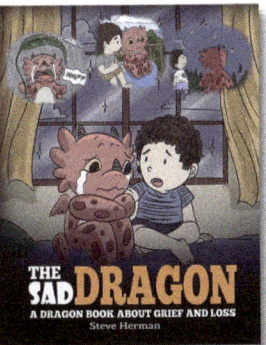  

  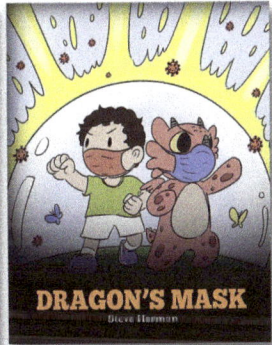  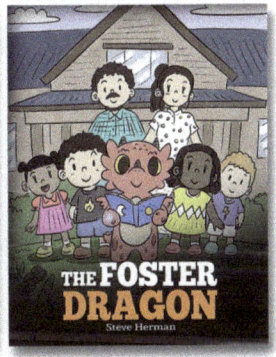
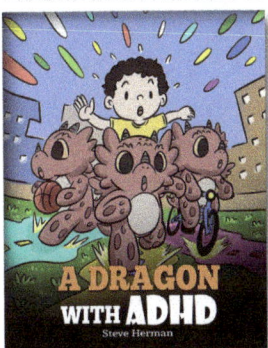    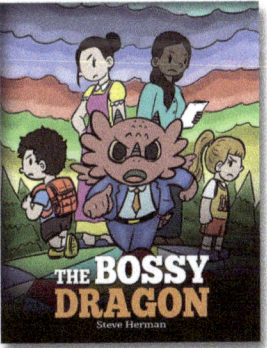
   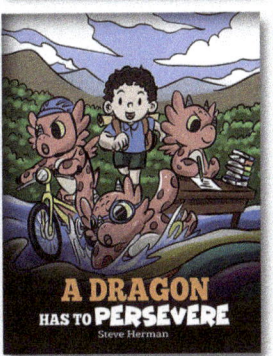 

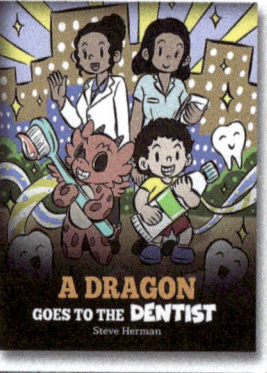

GET YOUR FREE GIFT AT
WWW.MYDRAGONBOOKS.COM/GIFT

Printed in the USA
CPSIA information can be obtained
at www.ICGtesting.com
LVHW061759191123
764328LV00013B/916